WHY BEAR HAS A STUMPY TAIL

AND OTHER CREATION STORIES FROM AROUND THE WORLD

Retold by
ANN PILLING

Illustrated by
MICHAEL FOREMAN

--→>•<←--

CONTENTS

--→>•<←--

WALKER BOOKS
AND SUBSIDIARIES
LONDON • BOSTON • SYDNEY

WHY SNAKE HAS NO LEGS

AN ASHANTI STORY FROM GHANA

WHEN THE WORLD WAS still very new all the animals had legs, except for Snail and he didn't mind because he had a snug little house on his back. All the others had to build their own shelters and they had to feed themselves, too, and grow things.

One day they decided to build a new farm and plant extra crops. It meant clearing a great big space in the forest and this was hard work, so they agreed to do it together and to share the harvest. But on the first day Snake, who was a bit of an idle fellow, said his great aunt was coming to see him and he would have to stay at home. The other animals went off to begin cutting the trees down and by nightfall they'd made a good start.

It was no thanks to Snake, though; he really was lazy. Next morning he said he couldn't help because his old

5

mother was sick and needed a visit. On the next day he said he had a bad cold. Every morning brought a new excuse. The animals grew tired of him, especially when he clambered up a tree and sat watching them all work, being critical and telling them they were doing everything wrong. "Come down and help us, then!" they shouted. But he just walked away, to another quiet spot.

All the animals worked hard and at last the crops were planted. After a time the rains came and everything sprouted, including a lot of weeds. But the animals were

good farmers; they dug and weeded and hoed, and at last a wonderful harvest was ready to gather in. All their hard work had been worthwhile.

But the night before they were to reap the first crop a terrible thing happened. Someone got into their plantation and stole it. And this happened again and again, night after night. The poor animals were heart-broken and they sent for the spider, Kwaku Ananse, because, of all creatures, he was by far the cleverest. He listened very carefully and had a long think.

Then he said, "Don't worry, I have a plan. Just be patient and in a week's time you'll have caught this thief, I promise."

Ananse went home and asked his son Ntikuma to help him. Together they collected up some barrels of tar and when it was night, they rolled them to the animals' new farm and spread the tar in great patches all around the ripest crops. Then son Ntikuma was sent home to bed. Father Ananse climbed into a tree and kept watch.

It grew very still and silent, and the spider nearly fell asleep, but then, just as he was nodding off, a loud noise woke him, a sound of grunting and heaving, a sound of someone cursing. It was Snake and he was stuck in the middle of a patch of tar!

Ananse slipped silently down from his tree and went home to his village, leaving the thief to struggle with the horrible stickiness. He knew Snake would never get free without some help. Serve him right, thought the clever spider.

Next day he summoned all the animals and they set off for their farm to see what had happened to Snake.

He was still stuck firmly in the tar but the other animals showed him no mercy. They grabbed long sticks and beat him till he squealed.

"Thief!" they shouted. "Fat lazy thief!" Then, stepping carefully between the tar patches, they went off to harvest the crops that were left.

Next morning they came back with some ropes. Ananse the spider led the way. They made a dirt path across the tar and tied the ropes round Snake. In those days he was short and fat. (No wonder, he just sat and watched other people work.) When everything was in place the animals pushed flat sticks underneath his body, to try and unstick him. "Pull!" Ananse shouted and they all tugged on the ropes. Nothing at all happened and Snake began to whine with fear. "Harder!" cried Ananse. "Pull harder!" So the animals pulled and pulled and PULLED.

For a long time Snake did not come out of the tar patch; he just grew longer and longer. Then there was a most peculiar sucking noise and, *Gloopity-gloop*, he was free at last. As he came whooshing out of the tar all the animals fell backwards on top of one another, in a heap.

There was silence for a minute or two, then everybody stared at Snake. He looked so very odd. What was wrong with him? What was different?

"He has no legs!" cried Ananse and, do you know, he had left them behind in the tar. That wasn't all – the stretching had made him terribly long and thin.

They carried him to his house and looked after him until everything had healed. Poor Snake sat and waited for his legs to grow again. But they never did. And that's why, nowadays, he has to go everywhere on his stomach, hiding in dark secret places because he is ashamed of himself.

->->-•-<-<-

How the World was Lit up by a Bonfire

-+> • <+-

AN AUSTRALIAN ABORIGINAL STORY

IN THE DREAMTIME, when there were no humans on earth, only animals, there was no sun. Everything crept about in a dim darkness.

One day, two birds, an emu and a crane, picked a quarrel. The fight was fierce and it raged for a very long time. In the end the crane snatched an enormous egg from the emu's nest and hurled it up into the sky.

She had thrown the egg so hard that it never came down to earth again. But somewhere up above, it hit a heap of firewood, burst open and dropped its yolk all over the sticks. This made a great fire blaze into life, a fire so big that it lit up the whole sky. For the first time ever the animals on earth could see.

A good spirit was watching them. Noticing how much happier the animals were, with light to see by, this spirit

decided they should have it every single day. So he gathered together all the other spirits and they set about collecting sticks which they heaped up into an enormous bonfire. The plan was to light a fire in the sky every morning, so that the creatures on earth could see properly.

Knowing that they might be frightened by this sudden strange light the good spirit first lit the morning star. He thought that when the animals saw it they would know the sun was about to shine.

But when the star appeared the animals were still fast asleep. So the spirit went to the kookaburra bird whose loud harsh cry could be heard above the voice of any other creature.

"Do something for me," he said. "When you see the morning star, cry out with all your strength. Your voice will wake up all the animals, and they won't be frightened when the new sun starts to blaze in the sky."

So the kookaburra opened his enormous beak very wide.

"Gou-gour-gah-gah!" he shrieked. "Gou-gour-gah-gah!"

All the animals stirred in their sleep, blinked round, stretched themselves and looked up into the sky. There was the gentle morning star and, as they watched, the sky turned slowly from black to grey, then to pink, then to red and gold, brighter and brighter as the flames of the huge bonfire licked at the dry wood, leaping up into a vast blaze

which lit the whole earth.

The fire grew bigger and hotter by the minute. The animals enjoyed the sun – the warmth of it and the light. They noticed that, at noon, the sky bonfire was at its biggest and hottest, and how, as the spirits let the flames die out, the earth became cooler and the light in the sky began to grow dim. In the evening all that remained was a dull red glow, which was sunset. Then the good spirit took some clouds and carefully wrapped them round the dying embers, putting them away in a safe place until the next morning, when he used them to start the fire again.

The kookaburra went on crying and screeching before sunrise, telling the world that the sun was about to come up and, when there were people on earth, mothers told their children not to laugh at him. He was so funny with his great big beak and his horrible voice. But they gave a warning. "If you say nasty things about Kookaburra," they said, "you will hurt his feelings. Then he might go away and sulk and if he did the sun wouldn't come up any more, ever again."

Think of that!

-+->-•-<-+-

WHY BEAR HAS A STUMPY TAIL

A STORY FROM NORWAY

ONE DAY BEAR MET FOX. Fox was slinking along as usual, his mouth stuffed with fish.

"Where did you get those fish?" said Bear. It was winter and food was hard to find. He was extremely hungry. He had never tried catching a fish but he was determined to learn. A few fat fish would make him a tasty meal.

"It's very easy," Fox told him. But he didn't like Bear very much and he decided to play a trick on him. "All you do is find a lake and slide across the ice till you reach the middle. You cut a hole and you sit down, and you stick your tail into the water. It stings a bit but you must leave it there as long as you can, because when it stings the fish will start biting. They're curious creatures, they'll soon come up to see what's happening. The longer you can stay there the more fish you'll catch. They'll hang on to your

tail. When you've caught some you just give it a little twist and out they come. Got it?"

"Got it," said Bear and he shambled off to find a lake. It sounded very easy. His mouth was watering as he banged at the ice with his huge furry paws and he'd soon made a nice big hole. Sitting on the edge, he stuck in his lovely long tail and waited.

Just how long he sat there Bear could never say. He grew so cold his rear end went quite numb. As for his tail, he couldn't feel it at all and there was no way of telling if he'd caught any fish. He got tired in the end, and stood up in a huff.

Snap! Bear peered down at the frozen lake. No fish. No tail either. It had frozen solid and broken right off. All he had left was a funny little stump.

-+->-●-<-+-

WHY RABBIT
IS SHY

Rabbit was not always shy. Once he was brave and fearless. Once, too, the sun was very different from the way he is now. He was much fiercer, if you can believe that! Here is the story of how they changed their ways, those two creatures Sun and Rabbit.

It happened long ago in the height of summer. No rain had fallen for many weeks. The rivers had dried up and the trees had withered. All day a huge sun shone down from a hard blue sky. The animals longed for clouds, and for rain to drop from them. They had no strength left to hunt for food. All day they crouched in the shadows of the brown trees and the baked, hard rocks, waiting for the end of things. It had never been so hot before.

Rabbit was as unhappy as the rest of them, but he was angry too. He shook his fist at Sun and shouted, "Go away, this minute! Stop shining for a while. Have pity on us. The earth is drying up. Can't you see what you are doing?"

But Sun took no notice at all. He simply went on pouring his red-hot beams down on the earth.

Rabbit stormed off and sat sulking behind a rock. Then he had a long think. "I know," he said at last, "I'll pick a fight with Sun and if he doesn't stop shining, I'll kill him."

So he set off for the end of the world, to the place where Sun rose each morning. He was bound to catch him there. He looked very fine in his hunting clothes, in his cloak of white buckskin and the skin of a coyote slung across his shoulders. On his back was a quiver of arrows, sharp enough to kill Sun, and he practised as he walked along, raising his bow to hit the cactuses and the yucca trees, throwing sticks at the ants and the beetles. By the time he reached the end of the world his aim was very good indeed.

But Sun was not there.

"Coward!" sneered Rabbit. "He's hiding. They must have told him I was on my way." So he hid in some bushes, and waited for Sun to come back. But Rabbit soon discovered that catching Sun was no easy matter.

In those days he came up in a rush – one minute it was dark and the next he took a great leap upwards, lighting the world in an instant. Rabbit knew that he would have to watch very carefully in order to catch him. So he fitted an arrow to his bow and settled down to wait.

Sun decided to play tricks. Rabbit looked so silly in his buckskin cloak and his coyote skin flapping round his shoulders. So he did not rise in his usual spot; he kept popping up all over the place, to the right, to the left, now in front, now behind. And however fast Rabbit drew his bow he always aimed too late. Sun had already escaped and was rushing away up the sky. "You'll never catch *me!*" he boasted.

Down below, Rabbit stamped about in fury. It was getting so hot the animals were dying. He too was growing weak, but he knew that he must be patient. Sun would get tired of playing tricks in the end.

Sure enough, after a while, Sun grew lazy and this gave Rabbit his big chance. Stealthily he crept out of hiding, drew his bow and released an arrow. It flashed through the air, hit Sun and went in deep.

Rabbit went quite mad with joy; he rolled about on the earth and gave great whoops of delight. He had done it! He had killed the sun! But after a minute he stopped whooping because he had seen something terrible out of the corner of his eye. Sun was bleeding, where Rabbit's arrow had pierced him. Flames were pouring out of a gaping wound in his side and everything seemed to be on fire. In trying to save the world poor Rabbit had made things worse. He really *was* going to die now.

Away he ran, and the fire swept after him.

"Help me, oh, help me!" he cried to the plants and bushes that lay in his path. "Give me shelter, hide me from these terrible flames."

But they all shook their heads. "We will be burned to ashes if we help you," they said.

Only the little desert brush was brave enough to give him shelter and that is why, today, it always turns yellow when the sun comes out.

Rabbit, too, changed colour. He got little brown spots on his neck where Sun scorched him, and he stopped being fierce and grew quite timid and shy. His fight with the sun had been much too much for him.

Sun changed too. He is now so harsh and bright nobody can look at him long enough to aim an arrow. But he is more wary than he used to be. He takes his time, these days, rising in the morning and setting at night. You never know. Rabbit might be waiting for him.

→►●◄←

HOW A CROW BROUGHT DAYLIGHT INTO A DARK LAND

IN THE FAR, FAR NORTH, where the Inuit live, it is dark for six months of the year and for the other six months it is light. This is the story of how that came to be.

At the beginning the Inuit did not know what daylight was because it was always dark. All they had to see by were little lamps of seal-oil. They never quite knew when they ought to get up and when they ought to go to bed.

One creature did know about light – he had seen it for himself as he flew round the earth. This was the crow, a friendly bird whom everybody liked and trusted.

"I've seen daylight," he said. "It's marvellous. You can see exactly what you're doing, you don't keep tripping over things. And of course, it's wonderful when you go hunting

29

because you can spot the animals a long way off."

The people's eyes grew round. Daylight was exactly what they needed. It would help them to see the great polar bears who came lumbering up out of the darkness to attack them.

"Go and fetch us some daylight," they said to the crow. "It would solve all our problems. We're tired of living in the dark."

At first the crow was doubtful. "I'm not sure," he said. "The land of daylight is many miles away and would they give me any if I asked?" But the Inuit begged and pleaded, so in the end he promised that he would do his best and away he flew, up into the eastern sky.

After a very long flight the crow noticed that it was getting lighter. He felt hopeful and flew a little faster, dropping down towards a village. Here the people still lived in igloos but the land was light. One of these igloos was bigger than the rest. It belonged to the chief and it was glowing with light. The crow slipped into the branches of a tree to see what was going on.

A woman came out with a bucket. He watched her walk over to the frozen river where she dipped it into a hole in the ice. As she walked back towards the chief's igloo, the crow turned himself into a little speck of dust and floated silently out of the tree. That was how he got inside. You don't often see a crow in a house, but there is always dust!

It was lovely inside the igloo. The chief sat watching his baby grandson play with his toys. These were very beautiful, all made of ivory: little boats called kayaks, carved polar bears and carved whales, tiny Inuit people and tiny igloos to put them in.

The baby laughed as he played at his grandfather's feet but then, quite suddenly, he screwed up his face and started to wail. A strange voice was whispering in his ear, and something was tickling him. "Tell them to give you some daylight," the voice was saying.

"Daylight," said the baby.

The chief brought down a carved wooden box full of his most precious things. Out of it he took a silver ball, rather like the ornaments hung on Christmas trees, but this was shinier than any of those. The baby grabbed it and started to chortle with happiness.

"Now ask for some string," whispered the strange voice.

"String!" said the baby obediently. And his grandfather tied a piece on to the ball for him, so he could play. The chief could refuse the child nothing. He was going to be very spoiled, when he got a bit older.

After a while the baby staggered to his feet and toddled out of the igloo into the wintry outside, pulling the silver ball behind him, watching as its wonderful shininess scattered the darkness with flashes of light.

The crow was ready. The speck of dust in the baby's ear

floated away and turned back into a handsome black bird which took the string in its beak and flew up into the sky.

The baby screamed as his marvellous new toy rose up into the darkness, the long string stretching out and the silver ball bobbling after it. The chief and his hunters shot

arrows at the crow as he flew higher and higher, but he was much too quick for them. On and on he went, breaking little pieces off the silver ball and dropping them on to the lonely dark villages below, so that each should have some light. When he reached his own village he dropped

the ball itself and it broke into hundreds of pieces. Every single house had light now.

"I could bring only one ball of daylight," puffed the crow. "All the daylight there is would have been too heavy for me to carry, I would never have reached home. So you will have to put up with darkness for part of the year. I hope that's all right?"

"It's wonderful!" everyone shouted and they ran about in the light, amazed at how easy it was to see things. The Inuit were great hunters but they never tried to harm the crow. He had done them a great service.

→>●<←

WHY ELEPHANTS LIVE IN THE JUNGLE

FROM THE KAMBA PEOPLE OF KENYA

THERE WAS ONCE A MAN who was terribly poor. His clothes were ragged and he had big holes in his sandals. He was always hungry too, because there was never any money to buy food. One day he went to see his witch doctor.

"I need some magic," he said, "some magic so I can make some money. I'm tired of being poor."

"Go and see Ivonya-ngia," advised the witch doctor. "He will help you, he's very rich indeed."

So the man tramped off to the village where Ivonya-ngia lived and found him surrounded by all his cattle. When he saw the poor man in his rags the rich man's heart melted.

"Give him goats," he ordered his men. "Give him sheep and cows. I have plenty to spare. That should give him a good start in life."

But the man shook his head. "I don't want your charity,"

36

he said ungratefully, "I want to become rich on my own. What's the secret?"

"Hard work," said the rich farmer.

"I just want magic," the poor man grumbled. He was in a hurry.

The farmer grew thoughtful. Then he dug amongst his robes and took out a little pot of ointment.

"Go home to your wife," he said, "rub this on her eye teeth, those two pointy ones in the top of her jaw. It will make them grow and when they're long enough you can sell them. They'll be pure ivory and that fetches a lot of money."

The poor man was greedy and rushed home at once, grabbed his wife and rubbed the magic ointment all over her pointy teeth. Then he waited. Sure enough the teeth began to grow. He sat there all day and all night, just watching her, his excitement mounting, with pictures of money bags floating through his head. And the teeth grew longer and longer.

At last they slowed down, then stopped altogether. When the man was quite sure the magic had finished its work he got some pincers and pulled out the teeth. Then he carried them to the market and sold them for a lot of money. He had become rich overnight.

The man next door was jealous. He was poor too, and as greedy as his neighbour. He went to see the same farmer straight away, came home with the same magic ointment, and rubbed it all over his wife's teeth. But he'd been in such a hurry to get rich he hadn't bothered to listen carefully enough to the farmer's instructions. He hadn't heard that he had to pull the teeth *out* and the silly man just let them go on growing and growing.

You can imagine what happened next. As the poor woman's teeth grew steadily longer, she herself began to change. Her skin became thick and coarse, her ears turned into two huge flaps and her nose became so long she could pick things up from the floor with it. She was soon so enormous that the walls of their little mud hut burst open and fell flat and, before long, she charged off into the jungle. You know why, don't you? Yes, she had turned into an elephant!

Soon after this she had a baby son and he was an elephant, too. She was much happier in the jungle without that greedy husband of hers back home. Elephants are wiser than people, and she never went back to him.

-+->-•-<-+-

WHY THERE ARE BUTTERFLIES

→>•<←

AN AUSTRALIAN ABORIGINAL STORY

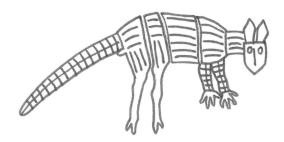

THIS HAPPENED WHEN THERE were only animals on earth. No people. And the animals were very happy because they did not know about death. But one day something terrible happened. A young cockatoo, who was just learning to fly, fell out of a tree and broke his neck. He lay on the ground like a jewel, all glowing against the greeny forest floor, not breathing, the warmth gradually fading from his feathers.

None of the animals could understand it. What was happening to the little cockatoo? Where had he gone? They all tried to wake him up, opening his eyes and prodding him very gently. But there was no life in him at all.

They sent for the owl, the wisest of all the birds, but he could not help them.

Neither could the eagle. All he did was to throw a pebble into the river. As it disappeared into the water he

40

cried, "See, it has passed from one existence into another. So has the little cockatoo."

So they sent for the crow. He took a stick and dropped that into the river. It vanished for a second but then bobbed up again. "There," said the crow, "we do not need to worry about death. We go into another existence like Eagle said, but we come back again."

The animals were comforted by this. At least death did not mean you disappeared for ever. But they wanted to know more. "We must put this to the test," they said. "Who will copy poor Cockatoo? Who will close his eyes and lie very still, not speaking or hearing or seeing or eating, for a long, long time, then come back to us, perhaps in some other shape?"

"I will," cried the snake.

"So will I," cried the wombat, the opossum and the goanna. And when winter came they all crept away, curled up in a dark warm place and went to sleep.

When spring returned all the animals gathered together and waited to see what had happened. The sleeping creatures came wandering along, very thin and dazed-looking. All seemed much the same except that the snake was wearing a different skin. Everyone was disappointed. This had not really solved the great mystery of death.

"Let us try," said the insects, the grubs and the water-bugs, the caterpillars and the beetles, but they were laughed at. They were so small and feeble, they had no brains at all.

"Well, you *can*," Eagle said doubtfully (he was in charge), "but I don't suppose you will get very far."

"Thank you, sir," said the insects politely and they crept away. The waterbugs wrapped themselves in bark and floated off down the river. Others crept into the trunks of trees or slipped into the ground. But before they disappeared they made a promise: "We will come back next spring in quite a different form," they told the larger animals. "Meet us in the mountains."

Winter came and everyone became sleepy and slow, but when the earth began to warm up again there was an excitement in the air.

One by one the animals began to travel towards the mountains. They met in a great clearing among the trees, which had already put out fresh green leaves in their honour. The dragonflies went all over the place, reminding everybody that it was time to greet the bugs and the caterpillars, who had promised to return in a new shape. Better still, they had promised to take away the awful terror of death.

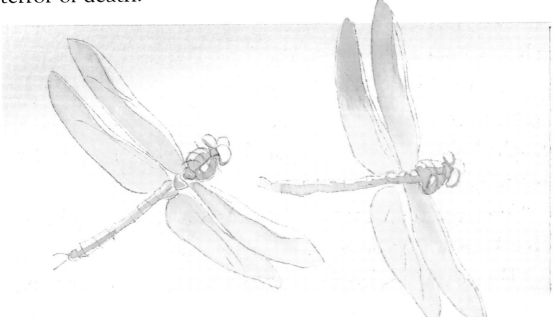

As the sun rose the animals which had gathered together in the clearing fell silent. The dragonflies were coming back but this time they were not alone. They flew at the head of what seemed at first like a great cloud of gorgeous colour – many, many colours, every colour on earth. As the cloud drew near it began to separate into smaller clouds and these clouds grew ever smaller, until they were mere puffs, like leaves, like specks of light.

Each one glowed with its own special brightness, and rested on trees and bushes and plants. The marvels were butterflies.

At first the watching animals could hardly speak; then they began to cry aloud, praising the creator of the butterflies, who had shown them that death was not dark and cold but that it meant new life.

And for the first time since the world began,
all the birds started singing.

Why Bear has a Stumpy Tail

Ann Pilling says that "In nearly all creation stories birds, animals and fish appear on earth before human beings, and they play important parts, sometimes showing more wisdom than mankind. But not always. Why for example does the bear, one of our biggest mammals, have such a silly little tail? Why are rabbits always so nervous and shy?" The stories in this book vary in mood, but all, she believes, have something to teach us, "because, like a good poem, a really good story 'begins in delight and ends in wisdom'".

Ann Pilling is the author of numerous books for children, including *Henry's Leg*, which won the Guardian Children's Fiction Award. She is married, with two sons and a grandson, and lives in Oxford.

Michael Foreman says that he loved doing the pictures for "these wondrous tales". He adds, "I have travelled through and sketched many parts of the world, marvelling at the amazing variety and contrasts of life on our planet. But what struck me most was how much all the people of the world have in common. Children are the same the world over. They all have a love of stories from Way Back When, when even the world was young."

Michael Foreman is one of the world's leading illustrators and has won many major awards, including the Kate Greenaway Medal twice. He divides his time between London and St Ives, Cornwall.

Some other Walker story anthologies

ISBN 0-7445-4366-5 (pb)

ISBN 0-7445-3771-1 (hb)

ISBN 0-7445-4438-6 (hb)

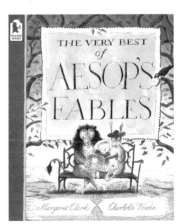

ISBN 0-7445-3149-7 (pb)

FOR THE BEST CHILDREN'S BOOKS, LOOK FOR THE BEAR.